SCIENCE MASTERS

EARTH'S PLACE IN SPACE

Tara Haelle

Rourke Educational Media
A Division of Carson Dellosa Education

ROURKE'S
SCHOOL to HOME
CONNECTIONS

BEFORE AND DURING READING ACTIVITIES

Before Reading: *Building Background Knowledge and Vocabulary*

Building background knowledge can help children process new information and build upon what they already know. Before reading a book, it is important to tap into what children already know about the topic. This will help them develop their vocabulary and increase their reading comprehension.

Questions and Activities to Build Background Knowledge:

1. Look at the front cover of the book and read the title. What do you think this book will be about?
2. What do you already know about this topic?
3. Take a book walk and skim the pages. Look at the table of contents, photographs, captions, and bold words. Did these text features give you any information or predictions about what you will read in this book?

Vocabulary: *Vocabulary Is Key to Reading Comprehension*

Use the following directions to prompt a conversation about each word.

- Read the vocabulary words.
- What comes to mind when you see each word?
- What do you think each word means?

Vocabulary Words:

- *axis*
- *core*
- *elliptical*
- *evaporate*
- *exoplanets*
- *friction*
- *habitable*
- *hypergiants*
- *matter*
- *probes*
- *revolution*
- *satellite*

During Reading: *Reading for Meaning and Understanding*

To achieve deep comprehension of a book, children are encouraged to use close reading strategies. During reading, it is important to have children stop and make connections. These connections result in deeper analysis and understanding of a book.

Close Reading a Text

During reading, have children stop and talk about the following:

- Any confusing parts
- Any unknown words
- Text to text, text to self, text to world connections
- The main idea in each chapter or heading

Encourage children to use context clues to determine the meaning of any unknown words. These strategies will help children learn to analyze the text more thoroughly as they read.

When you are finished reading this book, turn to the next-to-last page for **Text-Dependent Questions** and an **Extension Activity**.

TABLE OF CONTENTS

You Are Here 4
The Inner Planets 10
The Outer Planets 18
The Outer Reaches of the Solar System 24
Meet the Milky Way 30
Exploring Space 36
Activity 44
Glossary 46
Index 47
Text-Dependent Questions 47
Extension Activity 47
About the Author 48

CHAPTER ONE

YOU ARE HERE

Welcome to planet Earth! Since you have lived here all your life, you probably don't think much about what makes Earth special. But if aliens landed here, they would notice how Earth is different from other planets. For one thing, it is the only planet humans know of that supports life.

Earth is just a tiny speck in the vast universe.

How Big Is Earth?

If you walked in a straight line along the middle of Earth's surface (and could walk on water!) until you arrived where you started, you would walk 24,901 miles (40,074 kilometers). That's the circumference of Earth. The best known of these straight lines is the equator, dividing the northern and southern hemispheres.

You can walk along the Earth's equator near the city of Quito, Ecuador.

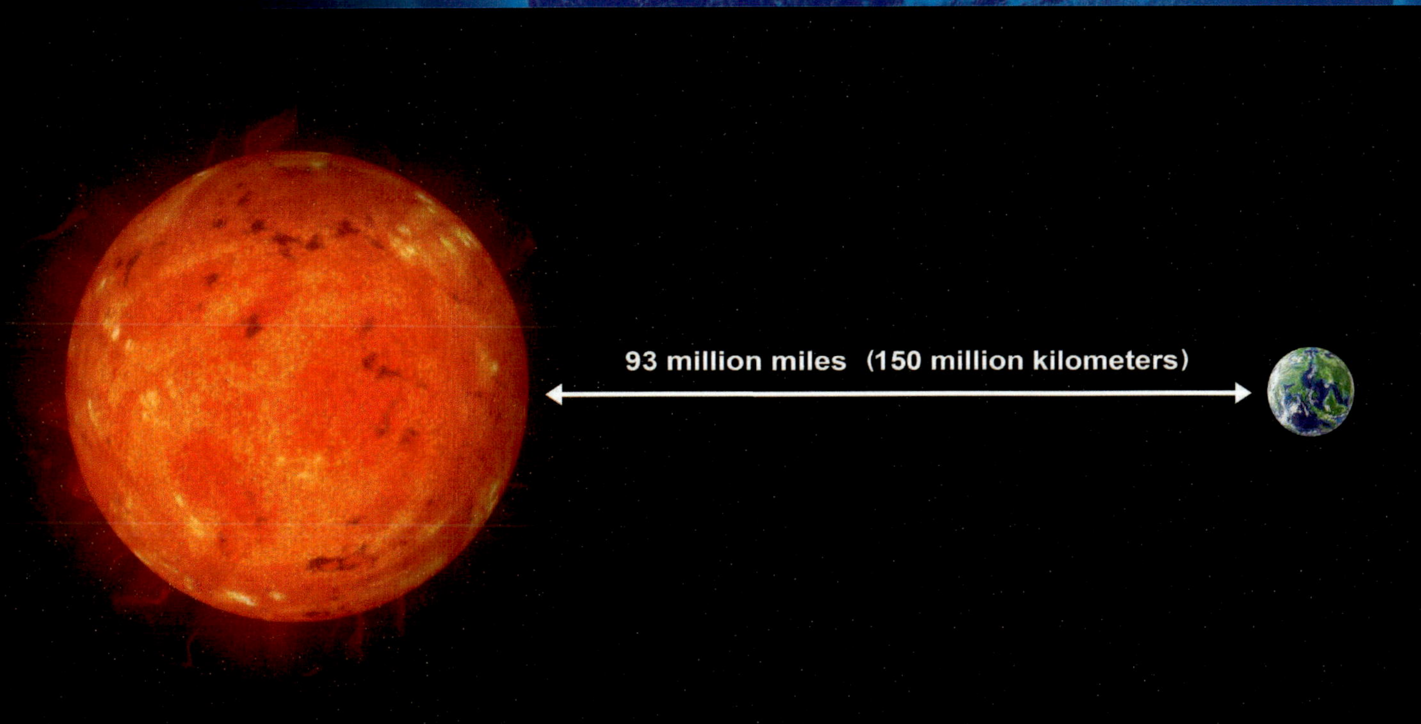

It takes about eight and a half minutes for the sun's light to travel to Earth.

Earth's features explain how humans and other life-forms thrive here. Two important characteristics of Earth are its distance from the sun and its plentiful water. Earth orbits the sun, a star, from about 93 million miles (150 million kilometers) away. That's close enough to provide enough light and warmth for life but far enough so that water does not completely **evaporate**.

Water covers about 71 percent of Earth's surface. If Earth were a pizza cut in ten pieces, seven pieces would be water. Pressure from Earth's atmosphere, a layer of gases surrounding the planet, helps to prevent too much water from evaporating or freezing.

Water makes life on Earth possible.

Earth's atmosphere is mostly made up of nitrogen and oxygen. These gases are critical for plant and animal life.

Scientists say that a planet is in the Goldilocks Zone, or **habitable** zone, when it is just the right distance from a star and has enough atmospheric pressure to sustain water. Since 1983, astronomers have identified at least 30 planets in this Goldilocks Zone. But no more than 12 are similar to Earth's size and are places where humans could probably live.

Light-Years Away

So far, all the planets scientists have found in the Goldilocks Zone are too far away to explore in person. Even the closest, Proxima Centauri b, is more than four light-years away. The unit that scientists use to measure distance in space is the light-year, or the distance light travels in one year.

It would take 17,000 years for one of today's space probes to reach Proxima Centauri b.

A planet's size and mass—how much **matter** it contains—determine how strong its gravity is. Gravity is the force that pulls things toward the center of an object. The more mass an object has, the stronger its gravity. Earth has about 80 times more mass than its moon, so Earth's gravity is much stronger.

Earth's gravity pulls objects toward its core.

Gravitational pull is a tiny bit weaker at the tops of mountains because peaks are farther from Earth's core.

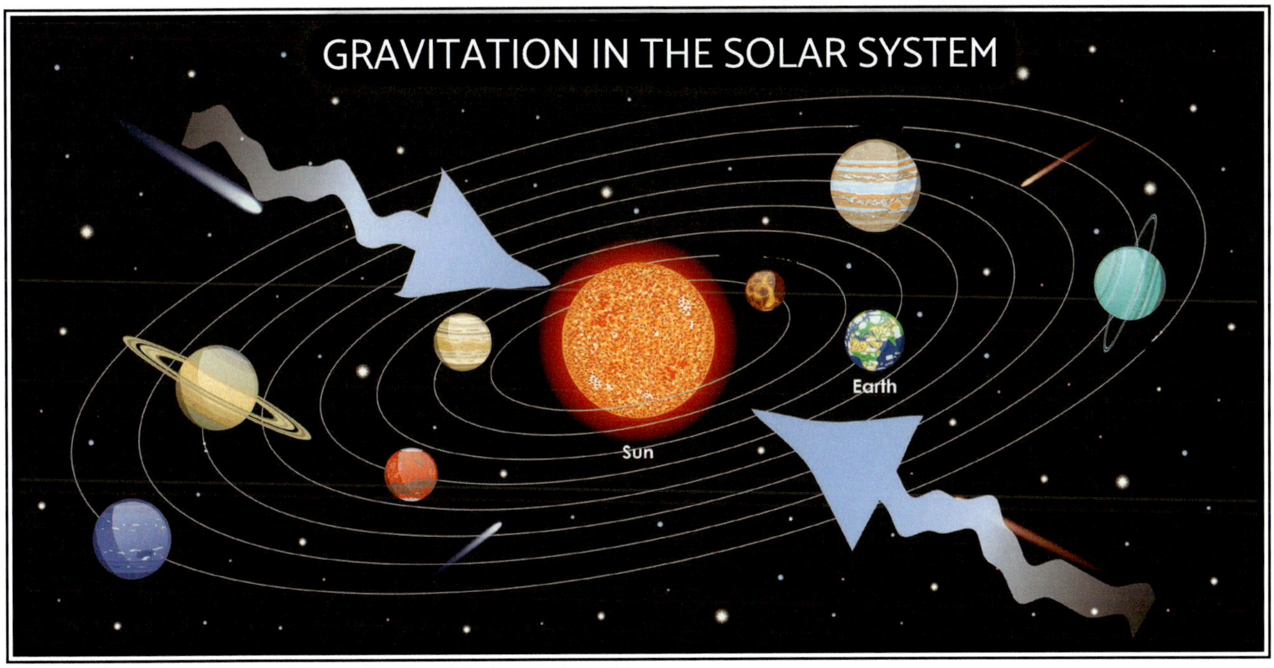

The sun's gravity keeps the solar system's planets in orbit.

But the sun's gravity is stronger than Earth's—and stronger than the gravity of every other planet in the solar system. In fact, the sun's gravity is what holds the solar system together. Throughout the universe, gravity is the force that holds together galaxies and other planets revolving around their own suns.

Long Shadows

When light hits an object it cannot travel through, it casts a shadow. The light's angle determines the shadow's length. Shadows appear short when the sun is high, shining straight down. But at dawn and dusk, the sun is low. Your body blocks more sunlight from the side, casting a long shadow.

Shadows are longer in winter than in summer because the sun appears lower in the sky.

CHAPTER TWO

THE INNER PLANETS

Earth does not orbit the sun alone. It is the third planet in our solar system of eight planets: Mercury, Venus, Earth, Mars, Jupiter, Saturn, Uranus, and Neptune.

The ancient Greeks suspected that the sun was a star. Scientists proved it in the 19th century.

The first person to suggest that the sun, and not Earth, was at the center of the solar system was the Polish scientist Nicolaus Copernicus in 1543.

Each planet revolves around the sun at a different speed. A complete **revolution** is one year, so the length of a year differs depending on the planet. An Earth year is 365.25 days. Every four years, the extra quarter of a day adds up to one whole day and gets added to the calendar as February 29, or "leap day."

What's in a Name?

All of the planets, except for Earth, are named for gods or goddesses in Greek and Roman mythology. Mercury, the fastest around the sun, is the Roman god of speed. Venus is the goddess of love, and the angry, red Mars is the god of war.

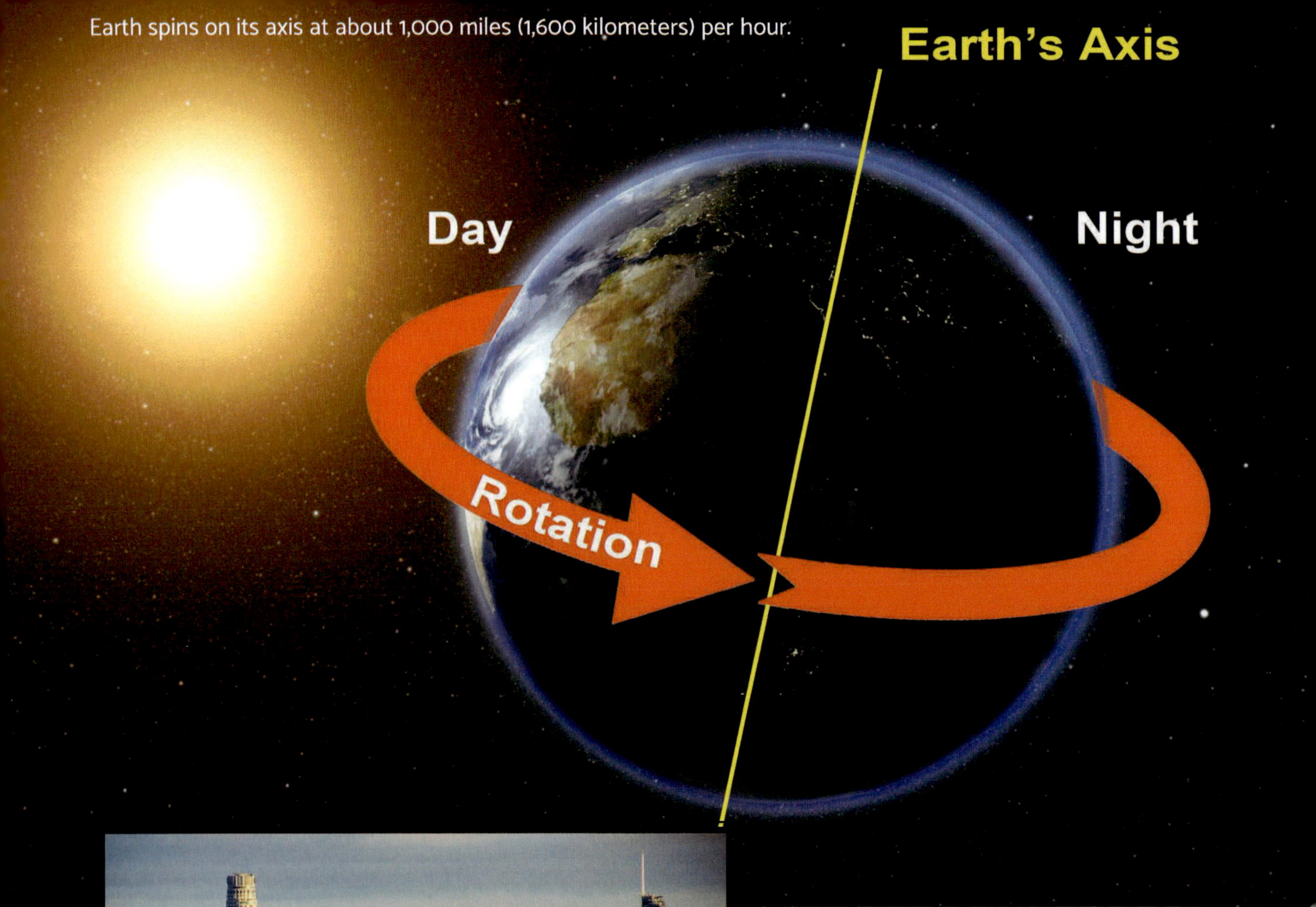

Earth spins on its axis at about 1,000 miles (1,600 kilometers) per hour.

Each planet also rotates on its own **axis** like a basketball spinning on a finger. The time it takes a planet to rotate once on its axis is a day, which is 24 hours on Earth. Earth's rotation gives us day and night. When a fixed point on Earth faces the sun, it is daytime. Night falls when that point rotates away from the sun.

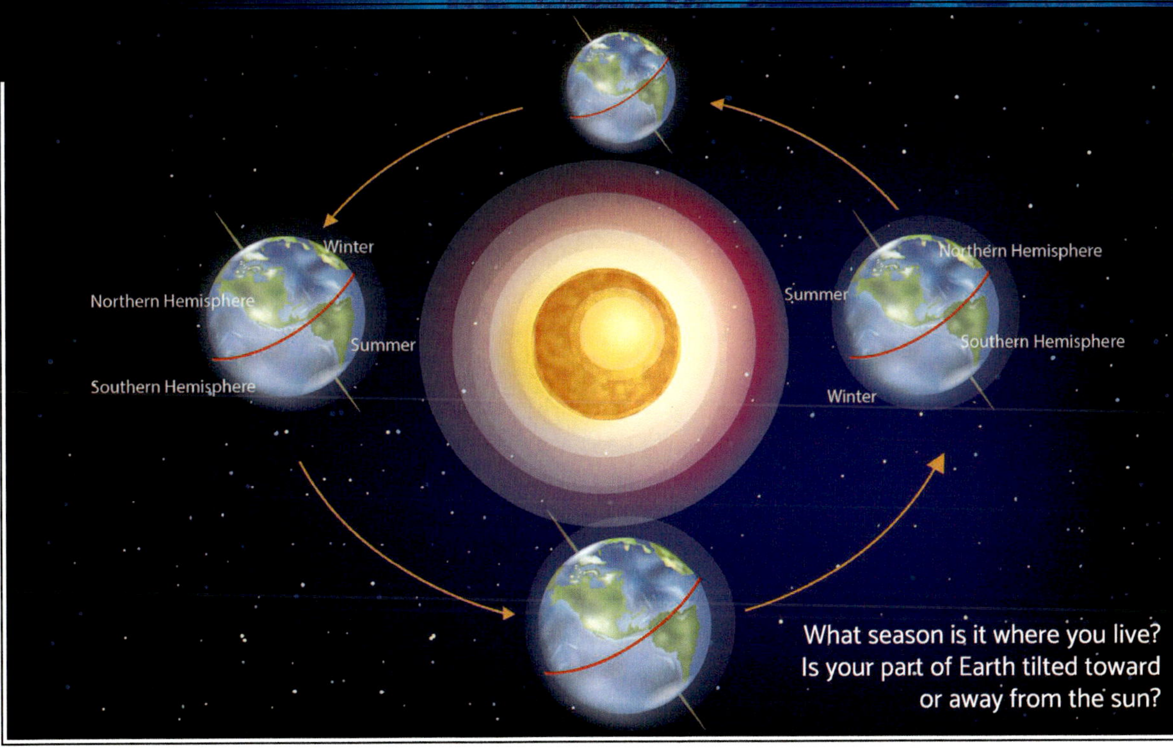

What season is it where you live? Is your part of Earth tilted toward or away from the sun?

But Earth's axis sits tilted. When the northern hemisphere is tilted away from the sun, it is winter there. Days are shorter with less direct light. When tilted toward the sun, the northern hemisphere experiences summer and its longer days. The length of actual daylight varies according to which hemisphere is tilted toward the sun and how far from the equator you are.

When Day Becomes Night

Sometimes Earth's moon crosses directly in front of the sun and blocks out its light for a few minutes, causing a solar eclipse. Similarly, a lunar eclipse occurs when Earth passes between the sun and moon, casting a shadow across the moon.

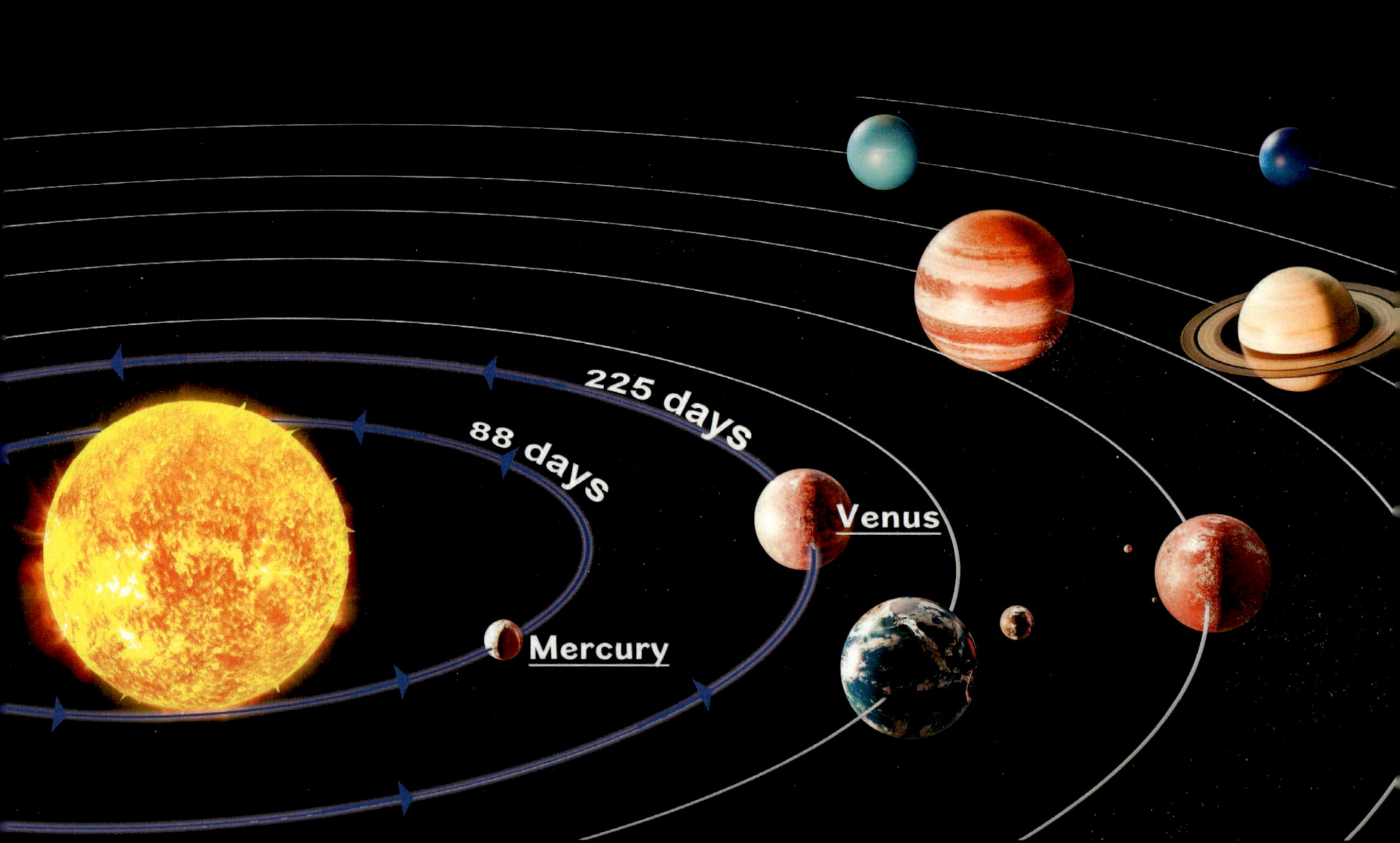

The closest planet to the sun, Mercury, takes 88 Earth days to make one orbit around the sun. By the time Earth completes one revolution around the sun, four Mercurian years have passed. But while Mercury's years are short, its days are long. Mercury takes 59 Earth days to rotate once.

Mercury Facts

- *A little larger than Earth's moon*
- *Rocky and cratered*
- *Thin atmosphere*
- *Temperatures range from minus 290 degrees Fahrenheit (minus 180 degrees Celsius) to 800 degrees Fahrenheit (430 degrees Celsius)*

How Long Is a Mercurian Day?

One Earth rotation includes a day and a night, but things aren't so simple on Mercury. Its solar day—one complete day-night cycle—takes 176 Earth days. On Mercury, a sunset only happens once every two Mercurian years!

Venus is the second planet from the sun. It is close to Earth's size but surrounded by a hot, poisonous atmosphere. Its year lasts 225 Earth days. Its day is even longer. Venus rotates backward from the rest of the planets, so its day takes 243 Earth days.

Venus Facts

- *Nearest to Earth and about the same size as Earth*
- *Thick atmosphere traps the sun's heat*
- *Hottest planet in the solar system at 900 degrees Fahrenheit (465 degrees Celsius)*
- *Has thousands of volcanoes*

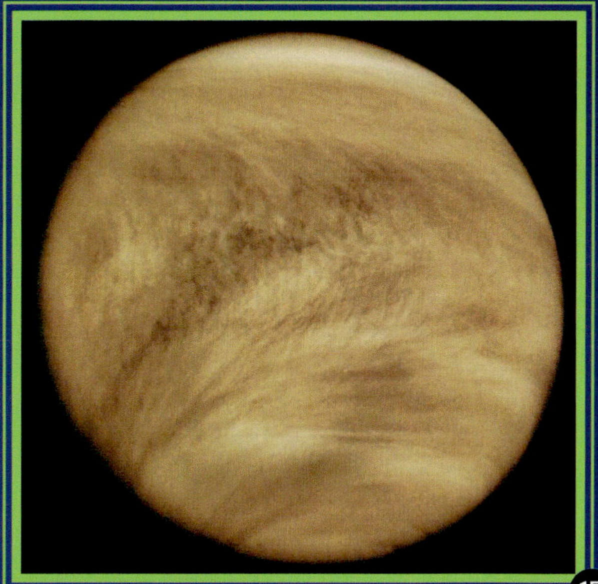

Mars has two moons, Phobos and Deimos.

Mars, the red, rocky planet after Earth, has a day similar to Earth's at just over 24 hours. But it takes almost twice as long—687 Earth days—to revolve around the sun.

Mars Facts

- *About half the size of Earth*
- *Appears red because iron in its soil has oxidized, or rusted*
- *Cold and desert-like with a thin atmosphere*
- *Some evidence of liquid water*

A Planet of Robots

Mars is the only planet whose entire known population is robots–our robots! The Viking 1 and Viking 2 landers arrived in 1976 to take photos of the Martian surface and study the soil and atmosphere. Pathfinder, Sojourner, Spirit, Opportunity, Curiosity, and Phoenix followed. In 2018, the InSight lander joined them.

Curiosity took this selfie with one of its 17 cameras.

The Viking missions were only expected to last 90 days. But Viking 1 (above) lasted over six years, and Viking 2 (right) lasted nearly four years.

CHAPTER THREE

THE OUTER PLANETS

The inner planets–Mercury, Venus, Earth, and Mars–are terrestrial, or land-based, planets. A robot could rove over them if it could withstand the toxic chemicals of Venus and the extreme temperature changes on Mercury. But the outer planets are made mostly of hydrogen and helium gases surrounding a small rocky or metallic **core**. These planets are called *gas giants*.

Asteroids can be as large as 329 miles (530 kilometers) in diameter. Some have their own moons.

The Asteroid Belt

Leftovers from the solar system's formation, asteroids are small, rocky objects that rotate with the planets around the sun. Most of the solar system's asteroids are found in the asteroid belt. This enormous field of asteroids is found between Mars and Jupiter. It divides the inner and outer planets.

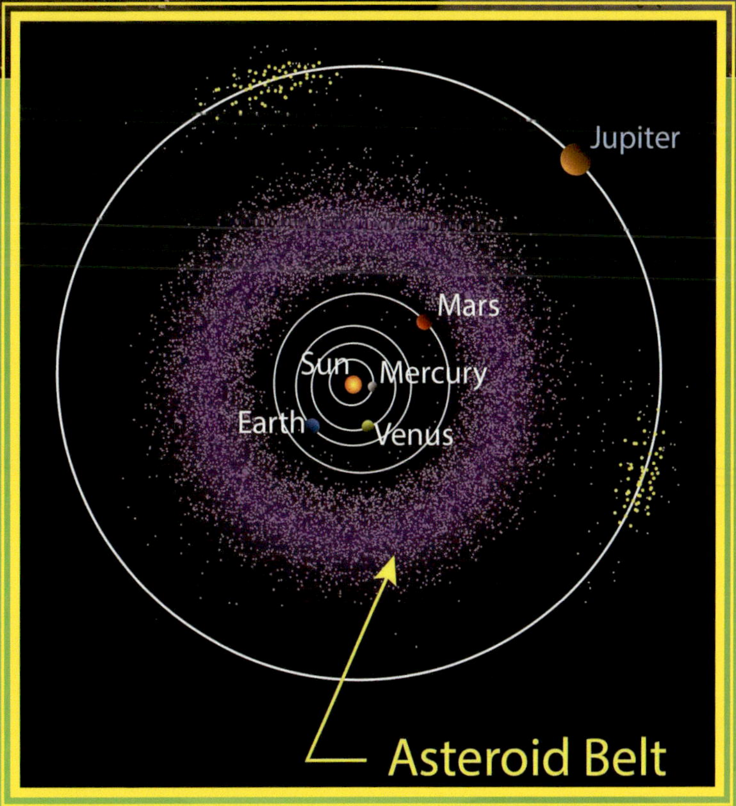

So far, scientists have counted 794,082 asteroids in our solar system.

The largest gas giant is Jupiter. It takes Jupiter over 4,000 Earth days to orbit the sun—that's almost 12 years! Its famous massive red spot is a storm twice the size of Earth that has raged for more than 100 years. Scientists have found 79 moons orbiting Jupiter.

Jupiter Facts

- *So big that 11 Earths could fit along its equator*
- *Solid core, if it exists, about half the size of Earth*
- *Rotates every ten hours*
- *Atmosphere made mostly of hydrogen and helium*

Saturn is best known for its rings made of ice and rock. All the gas giants have rings, but none are as large and spectacular as Saturn's. Its hundreds of rings make up seven major rings. It takes Saturn more than 29 Earth years to make a rotation around the sun. Saturn has at least 62 moons.

Saturn Facts

- *Nine times wider than Earth*
- *No solid surface, but might have a solid core*
- *About 886 million miles (1.4 billion kilometers) from the sun*
- *Cassini spacecraft orbited Saturn 294 times from 2004 to 2017*

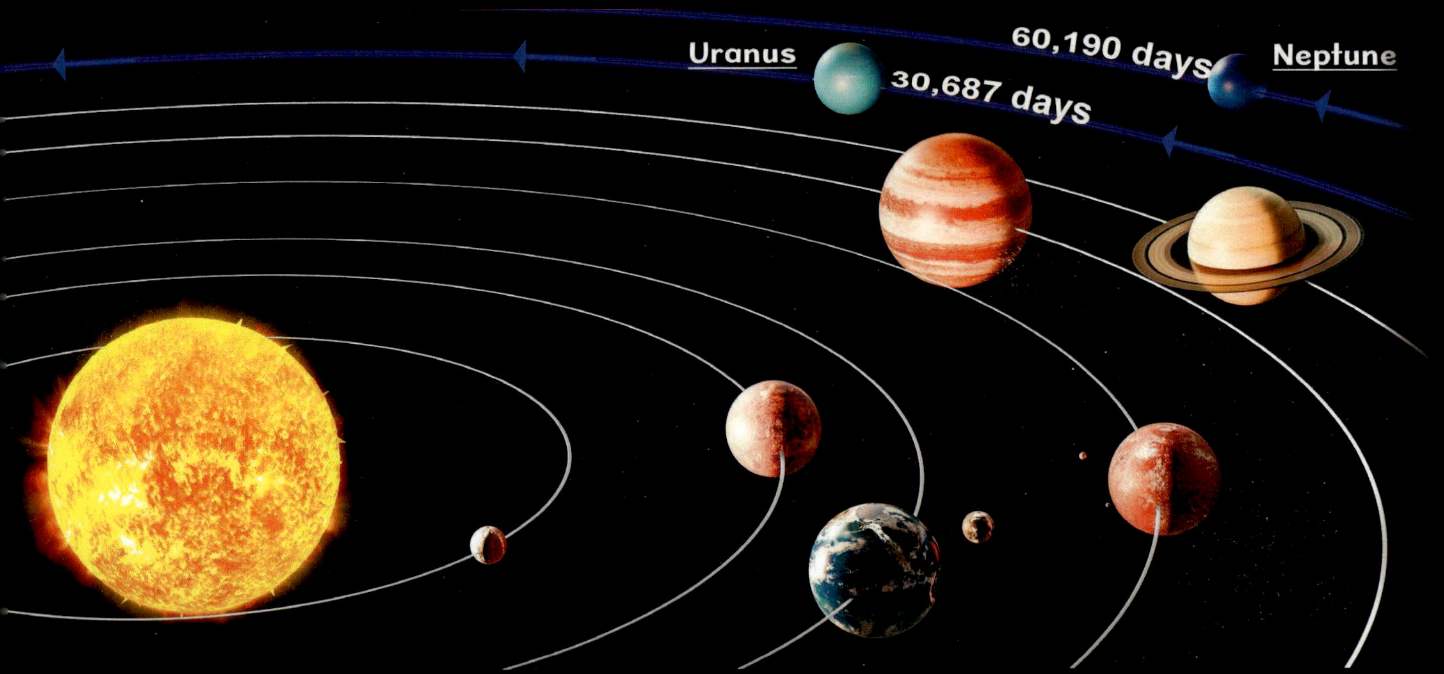

Uranus and Neptune are so far from the sun that their hydrogen and helium are largely frozen, making them ice giants. Uranus has 27 moons, all named for famous characters from literature. Like Venus, it rotates backward—and on its side! Uranus orbits the sun once every 84 Earth years.

Neptune spins far out in the solar system, about 2.8 billion miles (4.5 billion kilometers) from the sun. Its orbit takes about 165 Earth years. Its 13 known moons are named after sea gods and nymphs in Greek mythology.

Uranus Facts

- *About four times wider than Earth*
- *Blue color comes from methane in the atmosphere*
- *Rotates every 17 hours*
- *No spacecraft has orbited yet*

Neptune Facts

- *About four times wider than Earth*
- *Dense, icy water, methane, and ammonia around a small rocky core*
- *Has six faint rings*
- *Light takes four hours to travel from the sun*

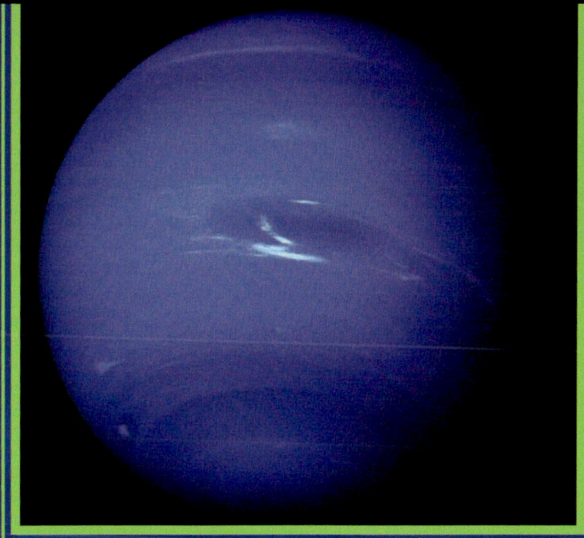

Where Can We Live in the Solar System?

Science fiction writers have long imagined humans living on Mars, on asteroids, or elsewhere in the solar system. Is it possible? Maybe. Some of Saturn's and Jupiter's moons might support life—several Jovian moons even have oceans. But the human body would have to adjust to different gravity environments.

Jupiter's four largest moons are Io, Europa, Ganymede, and Callisto.

CHAPTER FOUR

THE OUTER REACHES OF THE SOLAR SYSTEM

Planets and asteroids are not the only objects orbiting the sun. Dwarf planets are too small to be full-sized planets but too large to be called anything else. The International Astronomical Union, which approves names of space objects, defines a planet as a rounded body that orbits a star. But planets must also have orbits free of other objects. Dwarf planets have too little gravity to push away or pull in such objects.

Pluto, the largest dwarf planet, has blue skies and red snow.

Dwarf Planets

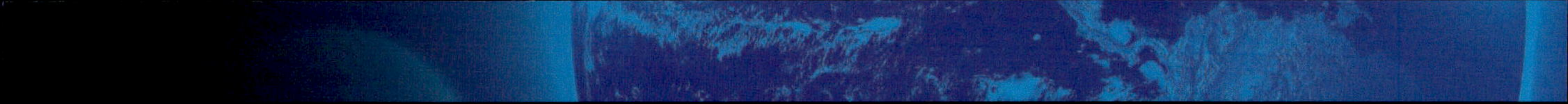

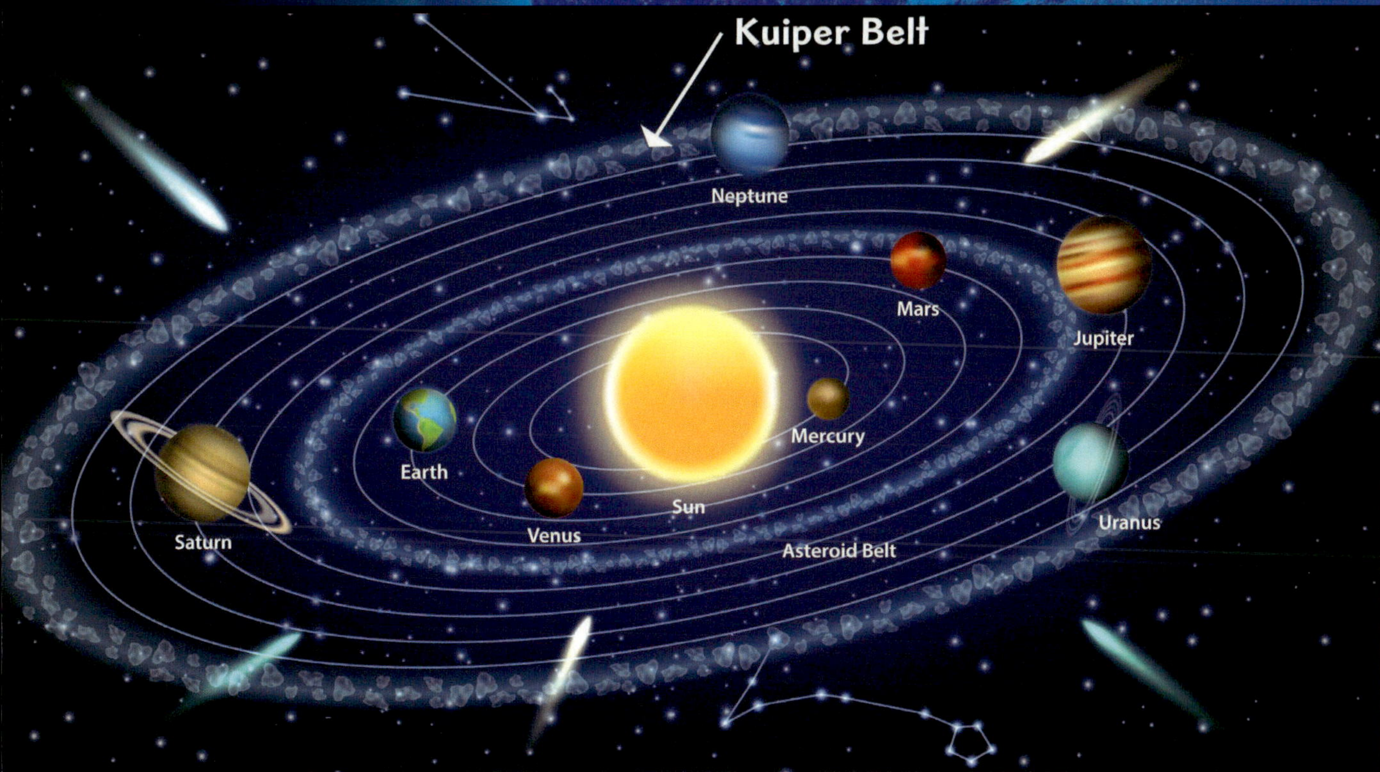

The Kuiper Belt lies beyond Neptune. New Horizons is the first space mission to explore it.

Ceres, Pluto, Eris, Haumea, and Makemake are the five officially recognized dwarf planets in our solar system, but hundreds of others may exist far out in the Kuiper Belt. The Kuiper Belt, a ring of icy objects just beyond Neptune, is where short-period comets are born.

Comets are icy balls of frozen gases and rock that leave behind a tail of glowing dust and gas as they orbit the sun. They are either short-period, taking less than 200 years to orbit the sun, or long-period, taking much longer.

Most comets are made of frozen water, ammonia, or methane.

Scientists estimate that up to a trillion objects may be found in the Oort Cloud.

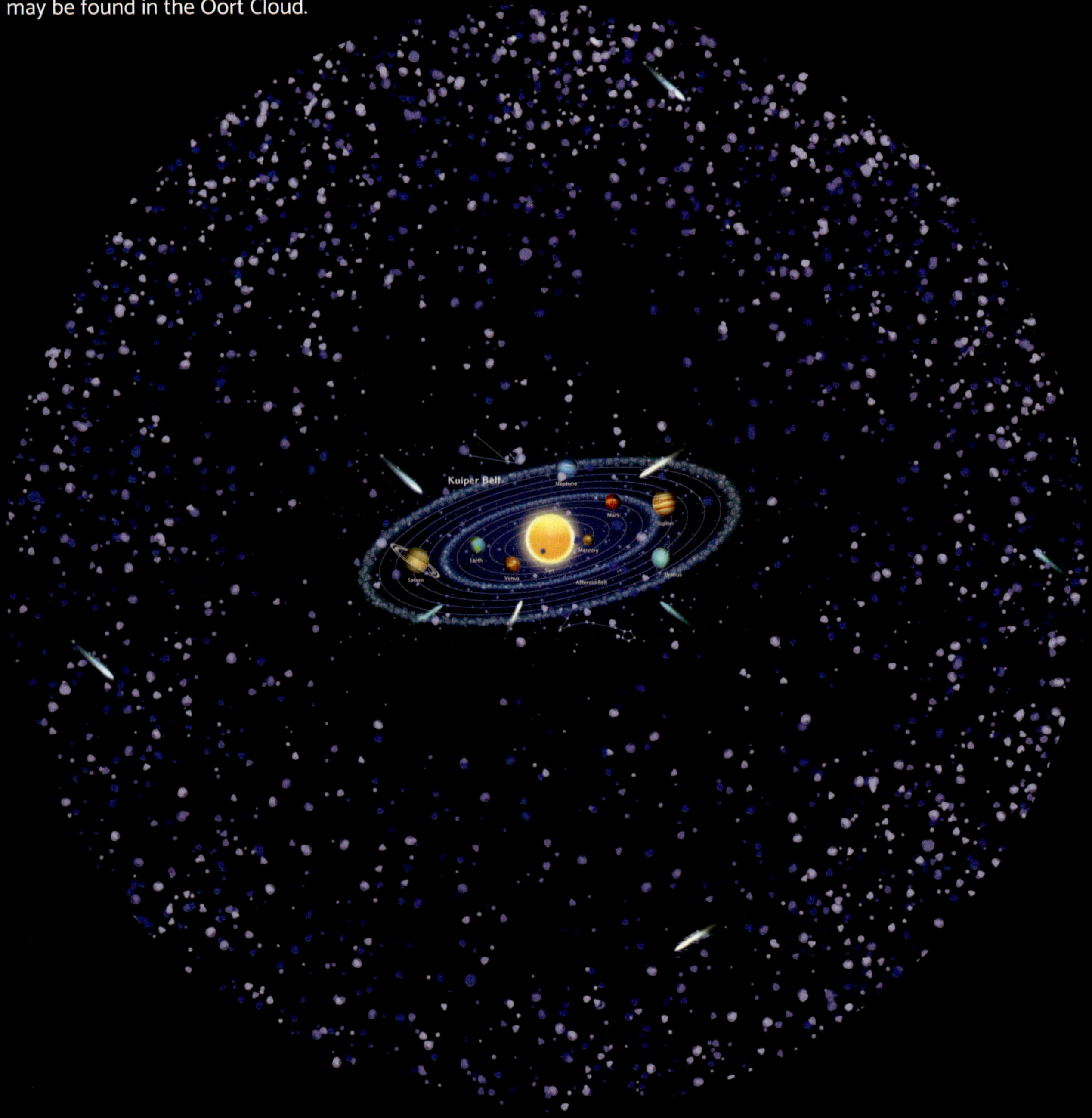

Beyond the Kuiper Belt is the Oort Cloud, the farthest part of the solar system still affected by the sun's gravity. This cloud of dust and icy objects is believed to form a giant shell around the entire solar system. It gives rise to long-period comets.

Most of today's adults learned in school that the solar system had nine planets.

Should Pluto Be a Planet?

Pluto was considered the ninth planet in our solar system until 2005, when Eris was discovered. Since icy objects remain in Pluto's orbit, the official definition of a planet left Pluto out. But not everyone agreed. When the New Horizons mission passed and photographed Pluto in 2015, debate flared up again. Some scientists want to reclassify Pluto as a planet.

Pluto is smaller than Earth's moon, but it has five moons of its own.

Have you ever seen a shooting star? It's not a star at all, but a meteor's fiery trip through Earth's atmosphere.

Littered throughout the solar system are pieces of rock called *meteoroids*. These become meteors when they pass through a planet's atmosphere. **Friction** from atmospheric particles burns up the meteor, leaving a fiery trail that humans see as a shooting star. Meteors that reach Earth's surface become meteorites. These range in size from pebbles to huge boulders that leave behind craters.

Meteoroids can be as small as a speck of dust or as big as an asteroid. They are made of rock and metal.

The Barringer Meteor Crater in Arizona is about 0.6 miles (one kilometer) across.

Meteor Showers

Every year, Earth passes through fields of debris that create meteor showers, when hundreds or thousands of meteors shoot across the sky. On a dark, clear night, you can watch these spectacular shows:

January–Quadrantids

April–Lyrids

May–Eta Aquariids

July–Southern Delta Aquariids

August–Perseids

October–Orionids

November–Leonids

December–Geminids

This is a fragment of the Canyon Diablo meteorites that caused the Barringer Meteor Crater.

CHAPTER FIVE

MEET THE MILKY WAY

The sun makes life possible on Earth, but it is only one star out of billions in the Milky Way, our galaxy. A galaxy is a massive collection of stars, planets, rocks, gases, and dust held together by gravity. The universe—the whole area of space we know about—is filled with billions of galaxies.

The Milky Way got its name because, from Earth, it looks like a puddle of milk spilled across the sky. In reality, it's a giant spiral with arms that rotate around a massive black hole like a pinwheel.

The Milky Way is about 100,000 light-years across. It has four spiraling arms.

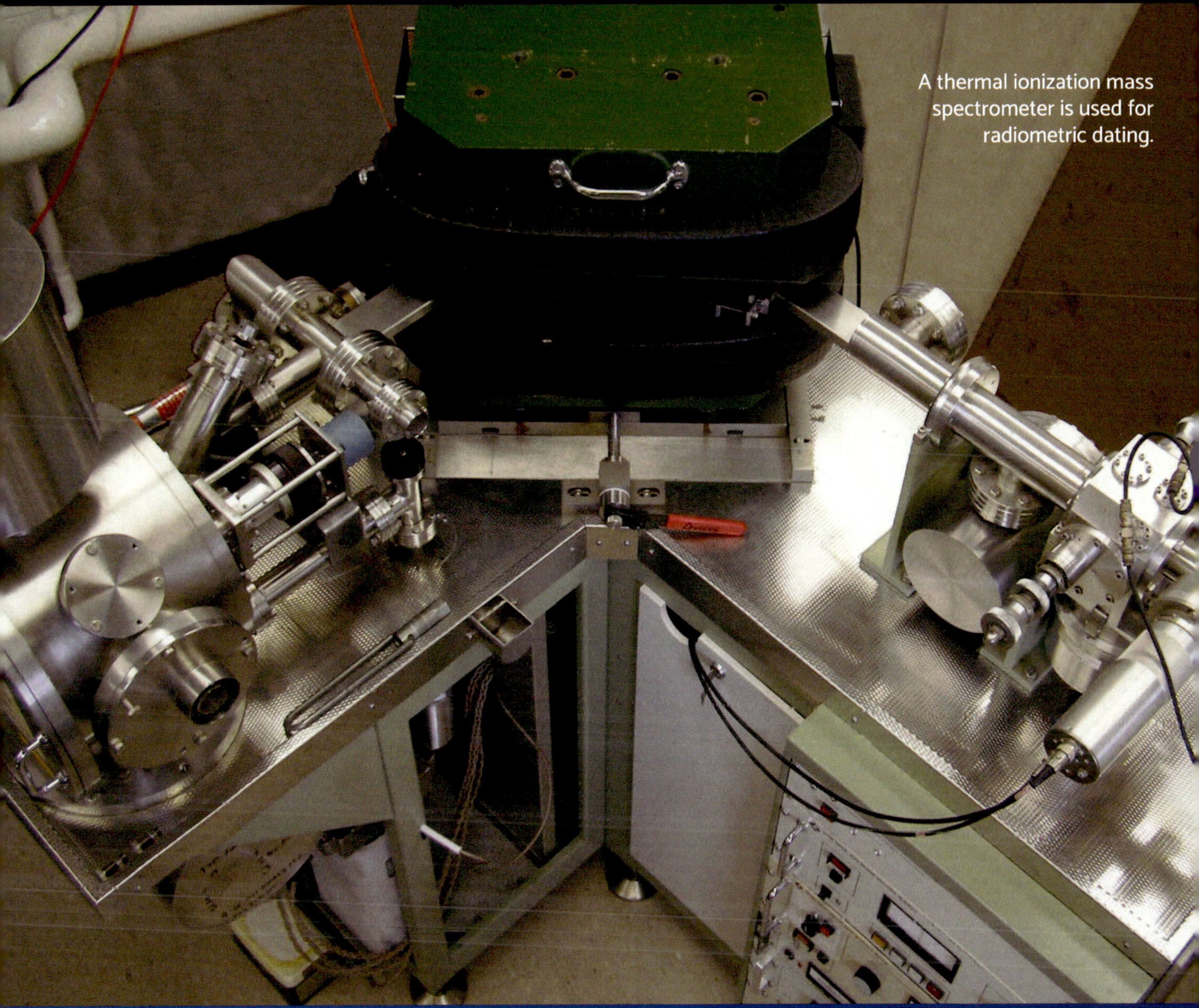

A thermal ionization mass spectrometer is used for radiometric dating.

How Old Is Earth?

Geologists have estimated Earth to be 4.54 billion years old using radiometric dating. Radiometric dating measures how much certain chemicals in Earth's oldest rocks have decayed over time. Scientists compare the age of these rocks to rocks from the moon and to meteorites to estimate when the solar system formed.

The farthest supermassive black hole ever discovered has a mass about 800 million times greater than our sun.

A black hole, despite its name, is an enormous amount of matter concentrated in a very small space. Imagine squeezing the entire planet Earth into an area the size of a marble—that's a black hole. All that matter creates an immense amount of gravity that sucks everything, even light, into it. Black holes release energy by gobbling up stars.

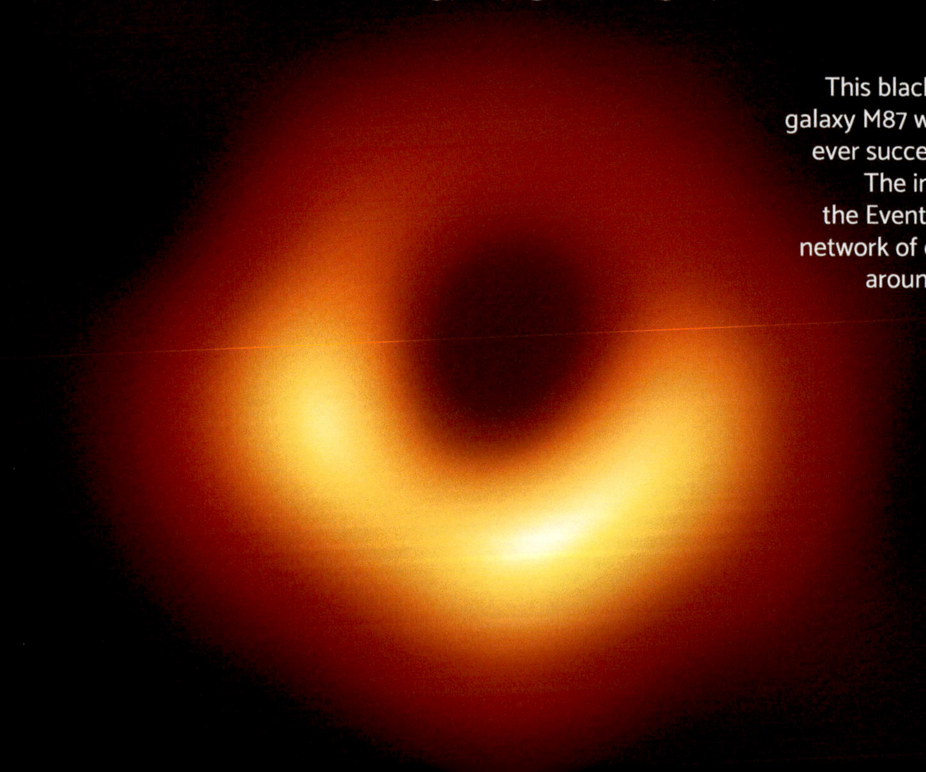

This black hole at the center of galaxy M87 was the first black hole ever successfully photographed. The image was captured by the Event Horizon Telescope—a network of eight radio telescopes around the globe operating together—in 2019.

Most black holes form from the death of a huge star in an explosion called a *supernova*. Stars can die in different ways depending on their size. Our sun will die by becoming a white dwarf, a gradually shrinking star that will eventually fade away.

Dr. Edwin P. Hubble
1889–1953

How the Universe Began

In the 1920s, American astronomer Edwin Hubble observed galaxies traveling away from us, going faster the farther away they were. This discovery confirmed that the universe is expanding. Scientists now theorize that the universe began 13.8 billion years ago, when a tiny hot stew of light and energy began rapidly cooling down and expanding, an event called the Big Bang.

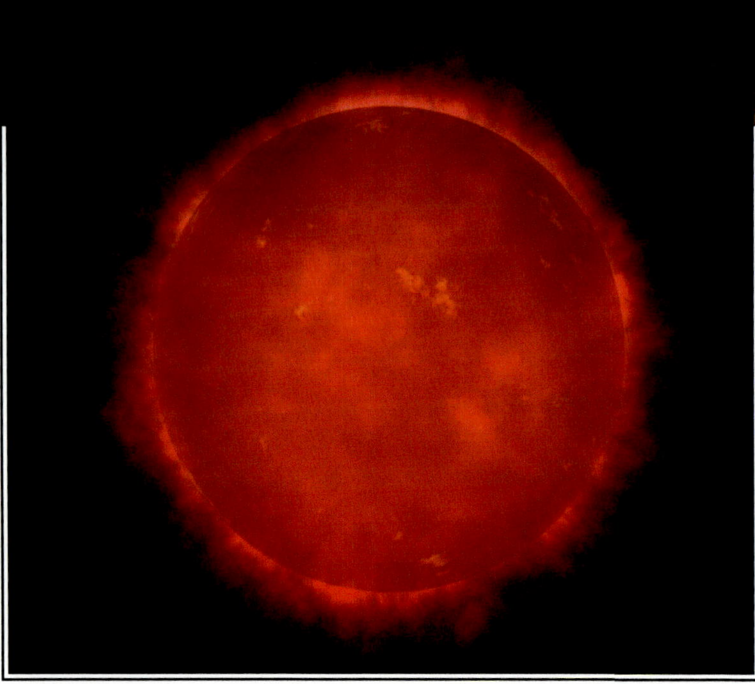

Star SO25300.5+165258, a red dwarf, is about 7.8 light years from the sun.

Leftover matter from dying stars often helps form new stars. Living stars range from small, plentiful red dwarfs to massive, rare **hypergiants**. From Earth, stars look like tiny pinpricks of light, but many are larger and brighter than our sun. They appear faint because they are so far away that their light must travel great distances to reach Earth. The sun shines so brightly, compared to other stars, because it is so close.

Stars gather into spiral galaxies like the Milky Way, or **elliptical** galaxies, which look like egg-shaped discs. Other galaxies are irregular, and are shaped like rings, like pencils, or have no clearly defined shape at all.

Most known galaxies are spiral.

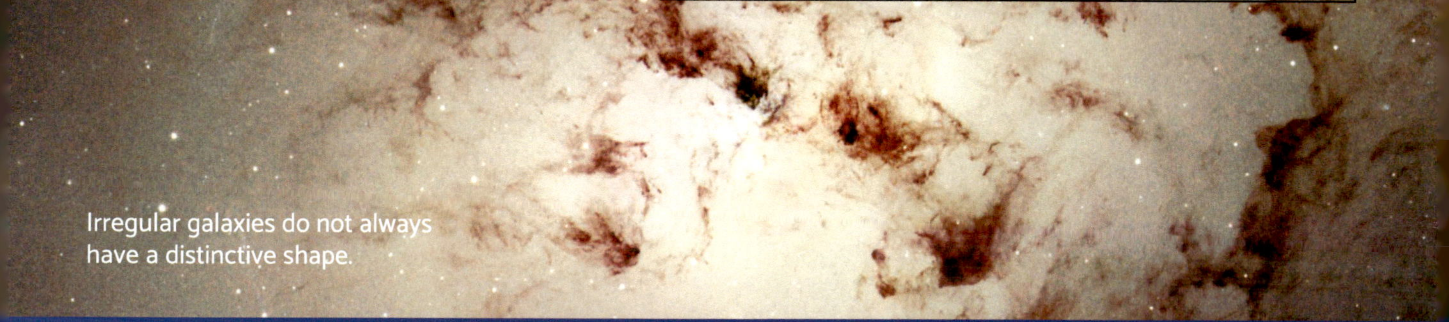

Irregular galaxies do not always have a distinctive shape.

Hubble's Picture of Andromeda

The nearest galaxy to the Milky Way is Andromeda. This spiral galaxy is more than two million light-years away, yet is visible in the night sky. Scientists have pieced together incredibly detailed images of Andromeda, like the one seen here, from photos taken by the Hubble Space Telescope.

CHAPTER SIX

EXPLORING SPACE

Just as the universe is expanding, so is human knowledge about it. As long as people have been able to gaze at the sky, we have wondered about its mysteries. But it was not until the 1950s that technology developed enough for us to launch objects—and later, ourselves—toward the stars.

Searching the Stars

As a girl, Jill Tarter gazed at the stars above Florida beaches. "Are we alone?" she wondered. Decades later, Dr. Tarter the astronomer is still wondering. As a director at the SETI (Search for Extraterrestrial Intelligence) Institute, she led a search of 750 nearby star systems for signals from space. The project used telescopes in Australia, West Virginia, and Puerto Rico. No extraterrestrial signal was found—yet.

Dr. Jill Tarter
1944–

Though only about 23 inches (60 centimeters) in diameter, Sputnik 1 weighed 184 pounds (83.5 kilograms).

The Soviet Union successfully launched Sputnik I, a beach ball-sized **satellite**, into Earth's orbit on October 4, 1957, kicking off a "space race" between the United States and the Soviet Union. The Soviet Union sent the first man, Yuri Gagarin, into space in 1961.

Yuri Gagarin
1934–1968

American astronaut Alan Shepard followed just weeks later. The United States was the first to put a person, Neil Armstrong, on the moon on July 20, 1969.

Alan Shepard was later the first person to play golf on the moon.

Satellites in orbit around Earth help us communicate, predict the weather, collect data about space, and more.

Since then, more than 550 people have gone into space, and more than 1,880 satellites have been put into orbit around Earth. More than 300 landers, rovers, and other **probes** have explored the solar system and beyond, often taking and transmitting photos back to Earth before crashing into the sun or other planets.

In 2012, Voyager 1 became the first functioning probe to leave the solar system. Voyager 2 followed, and New Horizons is bound for deep space too. NASA (National Aeronautics and Space Administration) launched 135 space shuttle missions before ending the shuttle program in 2011.

Rockets help launch probes and satellites into space. Here, Voyager 1 lifts off in 1977. Thirty-five years later, still traveling, it left our solar system.

Many scientists and technicians work to get spacecraft ready for launch.

Space shuttle Atlantis, taking off here on December 2, 1988, was one of NASA's six shuttles.

Columbia space shuttle crew

Challenger space shuttle crew

Challenger and Columbia Tragedies

Sending people into space is dangerous. At least 18 astronauts have lost their lives on space missions. Seven died when the Challenger space shuttle exploded 73 seconds after liftoff on January 28, 1986. Another seven died when the Columbia shuttle broke apart while reentering Earth's atmosphere on February 1, 2003.

More than 225 people have visited the ISS.

Did you know that people are already living in space? The International Space Station (ISS), a scientific laboratory orbiting Earth, has hosted astronauts from across the world since 2000. NASA is preparing to send humans to Mars by the 2030s. After that, as the astronaut Alan Poindexter said, "It's part of our moral fiber to go off and explore."

Onboard the International Space Station, astronauts live, work, and conduct experiments.

Data from radio telescopes like these is used to look for signals that may have been sent by life on other planets.

Is There Life Out There?

One goal of human space exploration is to look for other life in the universe. NASA used the Kepler Space Observatory from 2009 to 2018 to search for ***exoplanets****, or planets orbiting stars outside our solar system. They found more than 3,800. Soon the James Webb Space Telescope will take over the search.*

Kepler found planets that orbit two stars, planets entirely covered by seas, and more.

ACTIVITY

MAKE A STAR WHEEL

Thousands of years before telescopes existed, people identified shapes in the stars by drawing imaginary lines to connect them. They named these patterns, called *constellations*, after mythological figures.

As Earth revolves around the sun and rotates on its axis at night, the positions of the stars appear to change. Astronomers recognize 88 constellations that rotate across the sky according to the seasons.

Some constellations are visible year-round, such as Ursa Major in North America and the Southern Cross in the lower part of the southern hemisphere. Others rise only in certain seasons. Orion is the easiest constellation to find in winter, and others include Canis Major, Gemini, and Cassiopeia. In summer, Lyra, Cygnus, and Scorpius are prominent. To find constellations in the sky, create your own star wheel.

Supplies

◊ internet access

◊ printer

◊ cardstock or plain paper

◊ cardboard (if using plain paper)

◊ scissors

Directions

1. Search online for *Lawrence Hall of Science* and go to the main website for the science center. Search the site for *star wheels*. Download the northern hemisphere star wheel, or whichever star wheel corresponds most closely to where you live. If this doesn't work, do an internet search for *northern hemisphere star wheel printable*.

2. Print the star wheel holder and the star wheel on cardstock paper. (Or, print on plain paper and paste the cut-outs to cardboard.)

3. Cut out the holder, the wheel, and the center of the holder.

4. Place the holder over the star wheel and fold over the edges of the holder so that the wheel can be turned in its holder.

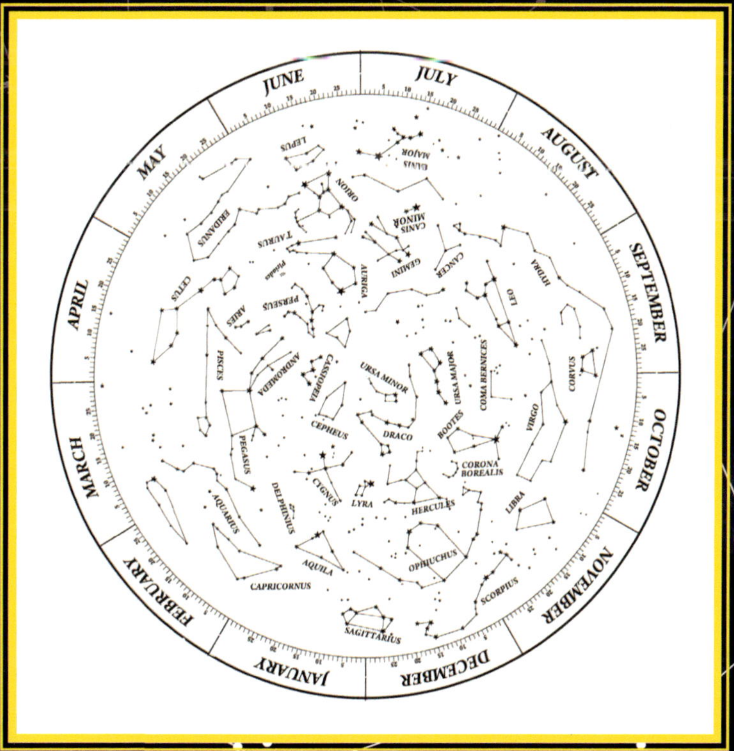

5. Turn the wheel to align the current month across the top of the wheel. Use your new star map to find the constellations above you on a clear night.

Glossary

axis (AK-sis): an imaginary line through the middle of an object, around which that object spins, as in Earth's axis

core (kor): the intensely hot, most inner part of a planet

elliptical (i-LIP-ti-kuhl): having a flat, oval shape

evaporate (i-VAP-uh-rate): to change into a vapor or gas

exoplanets (ek-soh-PLA-nits): planets that orbit stars that are not our sun

friction (FRIK-shuhn): the force that slows down objects when they rub against each other

habitable (HAB-i-tuh-buhl): safe and comfortable for people to live in

hypergiants (HYE-pur-jye-uhnts): the largest and brightest stars in the universe

matter (MAT-ur): something that has weight and takes up space, such as a solid, liquid, or gas

probes (prohbz): tools or devices used to explore or examine

revolution (rev-uh-LOO-shuhn): a complete movement of one object around another, such as of Earth around the sun

satellite (SAT-uh-lite): something in orbit, such as a moon that orbits a planet or a spacecraft in orbit around a planet or another heavenly body

Index

astronaut(s) 38, 41, 42
black hole(s) 30, 32, 33
dwarf planet(s) 24, 25
Earth('s) 4, 5, 6, 7, 8, 9, 10, 11, 12, 13, 14, 15, 16, 18, 20, 21, 22, 23, 27, 28, 29, 30, 31, 32, 34, 37, 39, 41, 42
galaxy/galaxies 30, 33, 35
Jupiter 10, 19, 20, 23
Mars 10, 11, 16, 17, 18, 19, 23, 42
Mercury 10, 11, 14, 15, 18
Neptune 10, 22, 23, 25
Saturn 10, 20, 21, 23
Uranus 10, 22
Venus 10, 11, 14, 15, 18, 22

Text-Dependent Questions

1. What is a shooting star?
2. What are the main planets of the solar system in order from the sun?
3. What does our galaxy look like?
4. What might make a planet habitable for humans?
5. How do astronomers determine the length of a day and a year on a planet?

Extension Activity

Pick out a star you can see from your home. Find out the name of the star. How far is it from Earth? What kind of star is it? Does it have any planets orbiting it that scientists know about? Pretend you have been assigned by NASA to learn as much as possible about that star. What questions would you want answered? What equipment would you use to learn the answers?

About the Author

Tara Haelle spent much of her youth exploring creeks and forests outside and reading books inside. Her adventures grew bigger when she became an adult and began traveling across the world to go on exciting adventures such as swimming with sharks, climbing Mt. Kilimanjaro, sailing the Nile, and exploring the Amazon. She earned a photojournalism degree from the University of Texas at Austin so she could keep learning about the world by interviewing scientists and writing about their work. She currently lives in north Texas with her husband, two sons, and a small menagerie of pets. You can learn more about her at her website: www.tarahaelle.net.

www.rourkeeducationalmedia.com

PHOTO CREDITS: Cover: Shutterstock | Aphelleon; Page 4-5: ©BDPub with NASA, shutterstock.com | Viorel Sima, shutterstock.com | Neosiam63863895, istock.com | alekseystemmer; Page 6-7: shutterstock.com | PopTika, shutterstock.com | studio23, shutterstock.com | ANON MUENPROM, ©ESO/M. Kornmesser www.eso.org; Page 8-9: shutterstock.com | Artur Balytskyi, shutterstock.com | D1min, shutterstock.com | Olinchuk, shutterstock.com | Rocksweeper; Page 10-11: shutterstock.com | Vectomart, shutterstock.com | AlexLMX; Page 12-13: istock.com | Senthilkumar Murugesan, shutterstock.com | Volodymyr Goinyk and BDPub, shutterstock.com | Sakurra, istock.com | Meowu, shutterstock.com | AlexLMX; Page 14-15: shutterstock.com | AlexLMX, shutterstock.com | Dotted Yeti; Page 16:17: NASA, shutterstock.com | AlexLMX, NASA, NASA/JPL; Page 18-19: NASA, istock.com | Mode-list, NASA/JP; Page 20-21: NASA/JPL, shutterstock.com | Dotted Yeti, istock.com | dottedhippo, NASA; Page 22-23: shutterstock.com | AlexLMX, shutterstock.com | 3drenderings, NASA/JPL, shutterstock.com | patrimonio designs ltd; Page 24-25: shutterstock.com | NASA images, istock.com | Meletios Verras, istock.com | SiberianArt, shutterstock.com | muratart;Page 26-27: shutterstock.com | AlexLMX/BDPub, istock.com | ChrisGorgio, NASA; Page 28-29: istock.com | dottedhippo, shutterstock.com | Marc Ward, shutterstock.com | Bjoern Wylezich, shutterstock.com | Action Sports Photography; Page 30-31: NASA, shutterstock.com | Denis Belitsky, ©Radiogenic/CC0 1.0 U.P.D.D; Page 32-33: NASA, NASA/JPL, Event Horizon Telescope collaboration et al.; Page 34-35: shutterstock.com | MichalPrzybylski, NASA/Walt Feimer, NASA/JPL; Page 36-37: NASA All except Dr Jill Tarter © Norwegian University of Science and Technology (NTNU). https://creativecommons.org/licenses/by-sa/2.0/; Page 38-39: NASA All; Page 40-41: NASA All; Page 42-43: NASA/JPL, shutterstock.com | Paulo Afonso; Page 44-45: shutterstock.com | Lia Koltyrina; Author photo © Darrell Lee Morehouse III

Edited by: Kim Thompson

Produced by Blue Door Education for Rourke Educational Media. Cover and interior design by: Jennifer Dydyk

Library of Congress PCN Data

Earth's Place in Space / Tara Haelle
(Science Masters)
ISBN 978-1-73161-467-4 (hard cover)
ISBN 978-1-73161-274-8 (soft cover)
ISBN 978-1-73161-572-5 (e-Book)
ISBN 978-1-73161-677-7 (e-Pub)
Library of Congress Control Number: 2019932384

Rourke Educational Media
Printed in the United States of America
07-3212511937